Trolls Don't Ride Roller Coasters

Check out all the books about

The BAILEY SCHOOL KIDS

ISBN-13: 978-0-590-18985-9
ISBN-10: 0-590-18985-9

27 26 25 24 23 22 21 20   14 15 16 17 18 19 20/0

Printed in the U.S.A.   40

This edition first printing, July 2007

Trolls Don't Ride Roller Coasters

by Debbie Dadey
and
Marcia Thornton Jones

illustrated by John Steven Gurney

Scholastic Inc.

New York Toronto London Auckland Sydney
Mexico City New Delhi Hong Kong Buenos Aires

For the two furry trolls in my house —
Tazz and Purrl — MTJ

For my special friends
Dave, Julie, Stuart, and Sarah Ewen — DD

Contents

1

Carnival

"Tonight's the night!" Eddie grabbed a limb of the oak tree and swung back and forth.

Howie grinned. "The carnival is my favorite part of spring. We're lucky we get to go on opening night."

It was after school on Friday and Eddie had met Liza, Howie, and Melody under the giant oak tree on the Bailey School playground. Melody jumped onto the limb beside Eddie. She hung upside down, with her black ponytail swinging.

"I'm glad our parents said we could go together. I can't wait to see the carnival's haunted house," Melody added before climbing down from the oak tree.

"I want to ride the carousel," Liza said,

clapping her hands. "All those painted horses are so pretty."

"Who cares about spinning in circles on fake horses?" Eddie asked as he dropped to the ground. He shoved his baseball cap down over his red hair. "This year the only thing I want to do is ride the Monster."

"What's the Monster?" asked Melody. "It sounds scary."

Howie nodded. "The Monster is built to be terrifying," he said. "I read all about it in the newspaper. It's the brand-new roller coaster."

Eddie grinned. "It's the longest, fastest, fiercest roller coaster ever."

"That's exactly why I don't want to ride it," Liza told him. "I'll just stick to the merry-go-round."

"We're too old for that," Eddie said. "This is the first year we can go on the roller coaster all by ourselves and I'm not going to let you stop me."

"The Monster is no ordinary ride,"

Howie said. "It has loops and spirals, and it even goes through a covered bridge called the Tunnel of Doom."

"That does it," Liza decided. "I'm not getting on that roller coaster."

Eddie grinned. "I'll make you a deal," he said. "If you ride the Monster, I'll go on your silly carousel."

"That's a fair deal," Melody said.

Howie nodded. "Our parents said we have to stick together. That means we all have to be willing to compromise."

Howie, Melody, and Eddie looked at Liza. "All right," Liza said. "But I hope this roller coaster is safe."

"Don't worry," Eddie said. "The ride will be over before you even have a chance to scream."

2

The Monster

"Follow me," Eddie yelled over his shoulder. Howie's dad had barely stopped the car in front of the carnival entrance when Eddie flung open the door and started running.

"What's the hurry?" Melody yelled after him.

"You said we could ride the carousel," Liza reminded him.

Eddie grabbed Liza's and Howie's arms so he could pull them along. "We'll ride the carousel later, but I want to get in line for the Monster," Eddie said. "Hurry!"

Liza, Melody, and Howie followed Eddie through the gate. The giant hills of the Monster loomed above the carnival like mountains. Eddie headed straight for them.

The four friends weaved around arcade booths and twirling rides. Liza slowed down to admire the painted horses when they passed the carousel.

"Can't you go any faster?" Eddie asked his friends. "I bet the line will be a mile long."

Howie nodded. "Opening night at the carnival is always busy."

"Everybody will want to ride the brand-new roller coaster," Melody added.

She turned and saw a sign on a post. "Check out this contest!"

Howie walked over to the sign and read aloud. "'Are you the strongest kid in Bailey City? Enter the Strongest Kid in Bailey City Contest on Monday night to find out. Winner gets to be first in line for every ride.'"

Eddie rushed over to examine the sign. "I could be the first in line for the Mon-

ster," he said. "All I have to do is win that contest."

Liza giggled. "But you're not the strongest kid in Bailey City," she told him.

Eddie puffed out his chest and held up his arms to show off his muscles. "Nobody is stronger than me," he said.

Melody laughed, but Howie patted Eddie on the shoulder. "If you're serious about entering the contest," Howie said, "then we'll be there to cheer for you."

"I'm serious," Eddie said. "I'm also serious about riding the Monster tonight. So let's go."

Eddie led them to the long line that snaked from the roller coaster. "We'll spend half the night waiting in line for this ride," Liza complained.

"It will be worth the wait," Eddie told her.

The four friends watched the Monster's cars *click-clack* up the first huge hill, then tip over the top and speed down the track, around loops, and into the covered bridge called the Tunnel of Doom. The cars made a deafening roar as they raced past the kids and finally slowed to a halt.

"Does it have to be so noisy?" Liza asked.

"It's the Monster's roar," Eddie told her. "The noise is part of the fun."

"That lady doesn't think so," Melody said, pointing to a little woman with bright red hair. She covered her pointed ears with her hands.

Eddie shrugged. "If she doesn't like the noise she shouldn't take up space in line."

"Maybe her best friend is making her ride it, just like you're making me," Liza griped.

Finally, it was their turn. The kids crawled into two cars near the front. They couldn't help noticing the tiny woman with bright red hair getting into the front car all by herself.

The four kids held on to the bar as the roller coaster *click-clacked* up the first hill. But the lady in front didn't hold on to the bar. Instead, she kept her hands over her ears. As the cars went flying down the hill, the breeze lifted her bright red hair straight up in the air. Melody screamed. Liza screamed. Howie screamed. Eddie just laughed and laughed as the ride thundered through spirals and around loops.

The roller coaster topped another loop, jerked around a corner, and then headed

straight for the covered bridge called the Tunnel of Doom. The *click-clack-click-clack* grew to a roar so loud that Liza couldn't hear herself scream.

The woman with wild red hair held her hands tightly over her ears as the ride zoomed into the tunnel.

Just then, the Monster screeched to a halt, and total darkness surrounded them all.

3

Evil

Liza screamed. Melody screamed. Howie screamed. Eddie laughed. It was so dark, the kids couldn't see their hands in front of their faces.

"Why are you laughing?" Melody asked Eddie. "This Tunnel of Doom is scary."

"There's nothing to be scared about," Eddie told her. "It's all part of the ride."

Howie put his hand on Eddie's shoulder. "I don't think this is normal. We've stopped." It was true. The roller coaster was absolutely still.

"It's broken," Liza whimpered. "We're trapped in the Tunnel of Doom!"

"AAAHH!" Melody screamed.

"Why are you screaming now?" Howie asked.

"Something just grabbed my arm," Melody gasped.

Liza giggled. "I'm sorry. That was me. I'm scared."

"Don't worry," Eddie said. "The carnival people will take care of us. They have to, it's their job."

Just then the kids heard a wicked laugh from the front of the roller coaster. It sent shivers up their spines and all the way down to their toenails.

"Oh, my gosh," Liza squealed. "Something evil is in here with us."

Suddenly a big flash of light came from the end of the tunnel. "Don't worry, folks. I'm the carnival manager. I'll have you out of here in a jiffy." A big man in a white jacket stood on a little walkway beside the cars. He held a huge flashlight. One by one he opened the cars and people climbed out.

"I'm not walking on that little bitty walkway," Liza said. "It looks dangerous."

Melody shrugged. "It's either that or stay in the Tunnel of Doom with whatever was making that weird laugh."

That was all Liza needed to hear. When the manager lifted her safety bar, Liza jumped onto the tiny walkway and started walking toward the end of the tunnel. She didn't stop walking until she got outside into the bright sunshine.

"Thank goodness I'm out of there," Liza whispered.

"It looks like everyone made it out," Melody said. "Only I don't see that little woman with the red hair. I wonder what happened to her?"

"Maybe she's already down," Eddie suggested.

"Down?" Liza said.

"Sure," Howie said, pointing to the long ladder beside them. It was over two stories tall and straight down.

"Wow," Eddie said. "One wrong step and you're a goner."

"I'm not getting on that!" Liza shrieked.

"There's nothing in this world that can make me do it!"

The evil laugh echoed out of the tunnel and the four kids looked at one another. Liza gulped and started climbing down.

4

Human Maze

"Let's go!" Eddie shouted. "I want to see if the Monster is fixed." It was a week later. Howie, Liza, Melody, and Eddie were on their way to the carnival.

"Oh, no you don't," Liza said, grabbing Eddie's arm. "You promised me you'd ride the merry-go-round and you still haven't done it."

Eddie slowed down and frowned. "You don't really expect me to go on that sissy ride, do you?"

Melody, Howie, and Liza nodded. "A deal is a deal," Melody said.

"Oh, all right," Eddie said. Eddie frowned the whole time he rode the merry-go-round, but Liza had a great time. She even sang along to the carousel music.

"Look," Liza said when her white horse leaped high in the air. "There's a human maze next door."

Eddie looked away from the tiger he was riding. "Cool," he said. "Let's do that after the Monster."

Liza shuddered. "We already went on that crazy roller coaster ride," she said. "Besides, it might break down again. I thought I'd die climbing down that huge ladder."

Howie shook his head. "I don't think

you have to worry about it. It's still not fixed." Howie pointed toward the Monster ride. A big sign said: OUT OF ORDER.

"Rats," Eddie said as the ride stopped. "How am I supposed to have any fun with the Monster broken?"

"Let's try the human maze," Melody suggested. The four kids ran into the maze and quickly got lost. Tall mirrors and wooden partitions made it hard to find the way out.

Melody giggled and put her hands against a mirror. "I feel like a mouse."

"What if we can't find our way out of here?" Liza whined. "I'm getting hungry. We could starve to death."

"Don't worry," Eddie said. "Follow me." Eddie turned. *Smack!* He ran face first into a full-length mirror.

Howie laughed. "Ooops! I don't think that's the way."

"Very funny," Eddie said, rubbing his nose.

Melody pointed to a short stone statue

beside another opening. "I think it's this way." The four kids paused in front of the statue. The statue had pointed ears and pointed hair.

"That's weird," Liza said. "This statue looks like that lady we saw last week on the roller coaster."

Melody gasped. "You're right. And look over there."

The four kids stared at five statues. Each one had pointy ears, pointy-toed shoes, and hair that stuck straight up.

"I have a funny feeling about these statues," Howie said.

"Me too," Liza said. "I feel like they're watching me."

"Ouch!" Eddie yelled. "One of them grabbed me!"

"Let's get out of here!" Melody screamed.

5

J.J.'s T-shirt Booth

Melody grabbed Liza and dashed around a corner. Howie and Eddie followed close behind. Every corner led them face-to-face with a stone figure. Finally, they found the exit. They ran out and tumbled to the ground, panting.

"That was worse than going through the haunted house," Melody said.

"I wasn't scared," Eddie said bravely. "They were only statues."

"If you weren't scared, then why did you run?" Howie asked.

"I wanted to hurry out of there so we could get some cotton candy and popcorn," Eddie said. "I was just joking about one of those statues grabbing me."

Liza frowned at Eddie. "I could use a treat after being scared half to death!"

Howie nodded. "There's a place right over there where we can get a snack," he said and pointed to a T-shirt booth nestled in the shadows of the roller coaster's Tunnel of Doom. A giant black umbrella protected the booth from the smallest dab of sunlight.

They were almost there when Liza stopped. "Look," she said. "That's the woman from the roller coaster."

Sure enough, the woman with the wild red hair was perched on a stool, only now her hair was stuffed under a giant straw hat. The counter in front of her was piled high with black T-shirts. On each T-shirt there was a picture that looked exactly like the statues they had seen in the human maze. The woman wore a T-shirt that was so short they could see her belly button.

"I don't like this," Melody said. "Maybe we shouldn't go over there."

"We can get popcorn someplace else," Liza added.

"Don't be ridiculous," Eddie said. "I'm hungry and I want to eat now."

"But there's something odd about that woman," Howie said. "She looks just like those creatures on the T-shirts."

"And in the maze," Liza said with a shiver.

"There is nothing strange about her," Eddie said, "and I'll prove it." Before his friends could stop him, Eddie marched right up to the strange woman and held out his hand. "My name is Eddie," he said. "We saw you on the roller coaster the other day."

The lady smiled, but instead of shaking Eddie's hand she squeezed sunblock from a tube and slathered cream all over her arms and hands. Then she rubbed some on her nose and chin. "My name is J.J. Trowlbridge," she said. Her voice was high and squeaky, like an old porch swing. "Would you like to buy a T-shirt?"

Eddie glanced at a shirt. "Why would I

want one of these creepy things on a shirt?" he asked.

J.J. frowned at Eddie. "These creatures are friends of mine," she said. And then she turned her back to Eddie to fold another pile of T-shirts.

Eddie joined his friends at the nearby candy counter. "She isn't very friendly," he told them.

"That doesn't mean anything," Melody said with a grin. "Lots of adults aren't very friendly to Eddie."

"You're right," Liza said, eyeing the cotton candy. "Let's get some candy."

The kids soon forgot all about J.J. They were giggling and talking about the rides they would go on next.

"SHHH!" J.J. hissed from her stool. "You children are too noisy. How am I to think with such chitchat, chitchat, chitchat?"

Liza closed her mouth. Howie turned red.

Melody said, "I'm sorry."

27

Eddie didn't bat an eyelash. He pointed to the roller coaster tracks. "Our noise is nothing compared to the Monster's roar you'll hear as soon as the ride is fixed."

J.J. scowled up at the tracks. "If I have anything to do with it," she said, "that ride will remain broken and silent forever!"

6

Tunnel of Doom

Howie waited until another group of noisy kids started fighting over the last bag of peanuts before pulling his friends aside. "I have an awful feeling," he said in a low voice.

"Then you better not go on any twirly rides," Melody warned.

"You shouldn't eat cotton candy," Liza said. "Cotton candy doesn't go with twirly rides."

Howie shook his head. "My stomach is fine," he said.

"Then it's all in your head," Eddie said with a grin. "We knew that all along."

"Very funny," Howie said, but he wasn't smiling. "I'm serious. There is something very wrong at the Bailey City carnival."

"I know," Eddie interrupted. "The best

ride of all time is broken, and nobody is even trying to get the Monster working again."

"Maybe it can't be fixed," Howie told him. "And if I'm right, we have more to worry about than a silent roller coaster."

"What are you talking about?" Melody asked.

"I'm talking about J.J. Trowlbridge," Howie said, his voice barely a whisper.

The kids looked at J.J. She sat behind the booth, rubbing globs of sunscreen onto her arms. Strands of bright red frizzy hair stuck out from under her straw hat. When the other group of kids laughed out loud, J.J. glared at them the way their teacher looks at Eddie when he talks during a test.

"I'll admit J.J. isn't the most friendly person we've met," Melody said, "but I don't think we need to be worried. There are lots of strange adults in Bailey City, and most of them aren't friendly when Eddie is around."

"We do need to worry," Howie told his friends, "because J.J. Trowlbridge is no ordinary adult."

"That's true," Liza said. "Ordinary adults don't sell T-shirts at a carnival."

"It's worse than that," Howie said. "Remember when we saw J.J. on the roller coaster?"

"I remember," Melody said. "That was the scariest ride of my life."

"And the noisiest," Liza added. "Especially when we went into that covered bridge. J.J. kept her ears covered, it was so loud."

"Exactly," Howie said. "Trolls hate noise on their bridges."

"WHAT?" Eddie yelped. "What do trolls have to do with Bailey City?"

"*Shhh*," Howie warned. "We can't let J.J. find out we know she's a troll or we'll be in big trouble."

"You already are in trouble," Eddie said with a laugh. "You're in trouble of being crazy."

"Trolls are made-up creatures from fairy tales," Melody reminded Howie.

"They don't sell T-shirts at carnivals," Liza said.

"And they definitely don't ride roller coasters," Eddie told Howie.

Howie looked at each of his friends before answering. "They do if they want to silence the roller coaster," Howie said slowly. "And J.J. has a reason for wanting the Monster silent."

"There isn't a good reason for wanting the Monster broken," Eddie argued.

"There is," Howie said, "if you're a troll living under the Tunnel of Doom!"

7

Crazy

"All that noise is driving me crazy!" J.J. complained to no one in particular. She was rubbing sunscreen onto her nose and frowning at a group of kids giggling near the merry-go-round. The Bailey School kids stood near J.J.'s stand, munching popcorn.

Liza looked at the merry-go-round. The carousel music sounded cheerful to her. "Let's ride the merry-go-round," Liza suggested.

Eddie nearly choked on a big piece of popcorn. "Not again," he said. "I almost died of boredom last time."

"It wasn't that bad," Howie said.

"I liked it," Melody said. "I want to ride a white horse this time."

Liza smiled sweetly at Eddie. "I'll give you the rest of my popcorn if you'll ride it."

Eddie grabbed Liza's bag and sighed. "All right, but you can't say I never did anything nice for you."　•

The kids raced over to the carousel. Eddie jumped on the biggest, fiercest-looking tiger. Melody got a big white horse with purple ribbons. Liza picked a little black pony with a pink saddle. Howie took the only animal left, a strange-looking creature with the head of a man, but the body of a horse.

"ROAR!" Eddie screamed. "I'm the king of the jungle."

Melody giggled. "You're the king of monkey business."

Eddie hopped up and down on his tiger, pretending to be a monkey. He chattered and grunted like a giant ape.

"Shhh," Liza said. "Maybe we should be quiet. J.J. doesn't like noise."

Eddie shrugged and grabbed his tiger's

ears. "Who cares what she wants. It's not like we're in a library."

"This is a carnival," Melody added. "It's supposed to be noisy."

"I guess you're right," Liza said.

Howie stared at J.J. She had closed her T-shirt booth and had walked over to the merry-go-round. She folded her arms and stared as the carousel started. The music got louder and louder as the merry-go-round went faster. Eddie grunted and Melody laughed out loud. Liza giggled, but Howie looked at J.J. As he passed her, J.J. threw back her head and laughed, too. Only her laugh didn't sound friendly. It sounded strange, almost wicked. Howie gulped. It was the same evil laugh they had heard on the Monster.

Instantly, the merry-go-round jarred to a halt as if something had broken. The ride stopped so suddenly, Liza almost fell off her little pony.

"What's with this place?" Eddie asked. "Everything is breaking."

Howie pulled Eddie away from the ride. Liza and Melody followed. "I know exactly what's wrong with this carnival," Howie whispered to Eddie. "And we have to do something before it's too late!"

8

Dolls

"I've got proof right here," Howie said. He lugged a big red bag under the oak tree. It was Monday and almost time for school to start.

"Proof of what?" Melody asked.

"That J.J. is a dangerous troll," Howie said.

Eddie pulled the bag away from Howie. "Are you still talking about little creatures with wild hair? It's bad enough that we have to go to school. Do you have to make it worse by talking about crazy stuff?"

"It isn't crazy," Howie said, "and if you open that bag you'll see what I mean."

Eddie opened the drawstring and reached into the bag without looking.

"AUGHHH!" Eddie screamed when he pulled out a small hairy item.

"Is it a mouse?" Liza asked, backing away.

Melody tried to see without getting too close. "Maybe it's a snake."

"Snakes don't have hair," Liza reminded her friend.

"I wouldn't be worried if it was a snake or a mouse," Eddie told them. "But this is much worse. It's a bag full of DOLLS!"

Howie nodded. "Trolls have lots of hair."

Eddie's face turned red and he dropped the troll onto the ground. "I can't believe I actually touched a doll. I think I'm going to be sick."

Melody ignored Eddie and peered inside the red drawstring bag. "These aren't normal dolls," she said. "They're trolls. Lots of kids collect them. Even boys!"

"You collect dolls?" Eddie asked Howie.

Howie held up a little troll that was as long as his finger. It had bright green hair and pointed ears. Instead of a belly button, it had a shiny red jewel. "These happen to belong to my sister," Howie said.

"I think they're cute," Liza said, picking a troll out of the bag and reading the tiny tag attached to its arm. "Each one has a little story to go along with it."

Melody pulled a few more trolls out of the bag. "These really do look like J.J.," Melody admitted. "Maybe she is a troll."

Liza shook her head. "All of these dolls have belly button jewels and J.J. doesn't."

Howie grabbed the red bag and dug around inside. In a few minutes he pulled out a different-looking doll. It was still tiny with strange red hair sticking straight up, but this troll wasn't smiling and it had evil glaring eyes. "This one has no belly-button jewel. Just like J.J."

"Ooooh," Liza said. "That troll looks mean."

"Wait until you read the legend," Howie said. "It gets worse."

Melody snatched the wicked-looking doll from Howie and read its little tag. "Oh, my gosh," Melody squealed. "We're in big trouble!"

9

The Legend

"'In the faraway hills of Scandinavia,'" Melody began to read, "'it is well-known that the good magic of jewel-bearing trolls turns the grass green, the sky blue, and the sun warm. The famed belly-button jewels give birds their songs, bells their chimes, and children their laughter. So good is the magic of the jewel-wearing trolls that they are welcomed into the homes and hearts of all.'"

"That sounds good," Liza interrupted. "It would be nice having trolls living in Bailey City."

"There's more," Howie warned. "Listen."

Melody continued reading. "'But beware of trolls without jewels, for they are grumpy and mean. Noise disturbs them,

so evil trolls spend their lives eliminating loud sounds. They have been known to silence cars, planes, and televisions forever. Fortunately, many areas are saved when the wicked trolls are turned to statues. Wicked trolls who foolishly attempt to silence loud noises when the sun is shining are often careless, letting warm beams touch their cold skin. If there is one thing an evil troll cannot stand, it is sunlight. The sun's warm beams thaw their icy hearts, turning evil trolls to stone.'"

"Don't you see?" Howie asked his friend. "That legend proves J.J. is a troll and she is living under the roller coaster bridge."

"The only thing that proves," Eddie said, "is that you still believe in fairy tales."

Liza nodded. "Eddie's right. It's only a story. Statues of evil trolls have nothing to do with J.J."

"Yes, they do," Howie said. "Remember the maze?"

Melody gasped. "The maze was full of statues!" she yelped. "And they all looked just like J.J."

"Exactly," Howie said. "I bet that maze is filled with evil trolls that tried to silence the world. Now the only troll left is J.J. And don't f scared of the sun. She stays under umbrella and she's always using sunblock."

"She did say those statues were like her friends," Eddie said slowly.

"If what you say is true," Melody said, "J.J. won't quit until all of Bailey City is silenced. We have to stop her!"

Howie grabbed the paper from Melody's hand. "'It is impossible to rid the land of an evil troll,'" Howie read to his friends. "'The only salvation is to trick the wicked troll into doing a good deed. Then the evil troll earns a jewel and becomes a good troll who travels the land doing kind acts.'"

Howie looked each of his friends in the eyes. "According to the legend, there is one way to save Bailey City," he told us. "We have to trick J.J.!"

10

Howie's Plan

"Your plan will never work," Eddie told Howie that afternoon. Howie's father had just dropped off the kids at the carnival and Howie was marching toward J.J.'s T-shirt booth.

"It has to work," Howie told Eddie.

"It won't work," Eddie said, "because J.J. isn't really a troll. She's just a crazy lady with wild hair."

"You might be right," Melody told Eddie. "But we have to try."

Liza nodded. "All we have to do is trick J.J. into doing a good deed. Besides, acts of kindness are what make the world a better place."

"I think acts of mischief are more fun," Eddie argued.

"Mischief causes trouble. Good deeds

help people," Liza pointed out. "By tricking J.J. we won't be hurting anybody."

"It will hurt me," Eddie snapped, "because I might not make it to the Strongest Kid contest in time, and if Ben wins I'll be in big trouble." It was a known fact that Eddie was always trying to prove he was tougher, stronger, and meaner than the fourth-grader named Ben.

"You'll get to the contest," Howie said. "But first, you have to help us turn J.J. into a good troll."

"Besides," Melody pointed out, "we'll be tricking J.J. and tricking someone is like causing mischief."

"Well," Eddie said with a grin, "maybe I can work a little fun into your plan."

Nobody was near J.J.'s booth when they got there. Since the Monster and the carousel were broken, her booth was surrounded by total silence. Even though deep shadows darkened the booth, J.J. rubbed sunblock onto her skin.

Howie stopped his friends. "We have to work together," he said.

Liza put her hand on Howie's arm. "Let me take care of this," she said. "I know all about good deeds."

Liza quietly walked up to J.J.'s booth. Howie, Melody, and Eddie followed close behind.

Liza stopped right in front of J.J. and sniffled. "Ahhh-chooo!" Liza pretended to sneeze. Then she sniffed some more. "Excuse me," Liza said. She made her voice sound all stuffy. "May I have a tissue?"

J.J. didn't have a chance to answer because Eddie pushed his arm in front of Liza's nose. "Here," Eddie said. "You can use my T-shirt!"

"Ewww," Melody said. "That's disgusting."

J.J. looked at Eddie. A tiny smile tickled the corners of her mouth before she turned away to fold more T-shirts. Liza

scowled at Eddie, but Eddie pretended not to notice.

Melody stepped between her two friends. "Leave it to me," she whispered. Then Melody started picking up T-shirts until she had a huge pile balanced in her hands. "I just can't decide which T-shirt I like the best," she told J.J. in a sweet voice. "Could you please hold these so I can make up my mind?"

Before J.J. could take the stack of T-shirts, Eddie squeezed between them. "Let me see those," he said. But when Melody handed Eddie the stack, he pulled his hands away and all the T-shirts tumbled to the ground.

Eddie laughed and J.J. chuckled. Howie took a step toward the counter and pre-tended to trip. "I'm falling," he cried, swinging his arms in crazy circles. "Help me! Help me!"

J.J. moved toward Howie, but Eddie beat her. He reached out and gave Howie a tiny shove. It was enough to throw

Howie off balance. Howie fell back and bumped Melody. Melody fell into Liza. All three of them landed in a heap on the ground. Eddie laughed so hard he doubled over. J.J. looked at Eddie and laughed, too.

Melody, Liza, and Howie untangled their arms and legs. Then they jumped up and stomped away from J.J.'s booth, and from Eddie. Eddie had to hurry to catch up.

"What's wrong?" Eddie asked in his most innocent voice. "You said tricking people was like causing mischief. I was just having a little fun."

"But you spoiled everything," Melody snapped.

Eddie shrugged. "I kind of like J.J.," he said. "She laughed when I goofed off. I think she likes me, too."

"Leave it to Eddie to make friends with a wicked troll," Howie said.

"You never proved she was a troll,"

Eddie pointed out. "I think you're being mean to her."

"We just wanted her to do something nice," Liza pointed out. "But we should have known better than to ask you to understand. You don't have a nice bone in your body!"

"That's not true," Eddie argued. "Besides, you're not being nice to me!"

"What are you talking about?" Howie asked. "We're still talking to you, and considering what you did at J.J.'s booth, I think that's pretty nice of us!"

"I'm talking about the Strongest Kid contest," Eddie said. "I don't want to be late."

"Late? Late for what?" asked a squeaky voice from behind them.

J.J. had sneaked up behind the kids. She stood in the shadows of her giant black umbrella.

Howie turned red. Melody and Liza were speechless. Eddie didn't skip a beat. "I plan to win the Strongest Kid contest,"

Eddie bragged. "I was depending on my friends to cheer louder than anybody else."

"Cheering?" J.J. asked in her squeaky voice.

Eddie nodded. "Every kid in Bailey City will be there to cheer and yell," he said. He was about to tell J.J. more, but she didn't give him a chance. Instead, she turned and stomped straight for the Strongest Kid contest!

11

Contest

"Where is she going?" Melody asked.

"It looks like she's going to the contest," Liza said.

"We have to follow her," Howie added.

"No," Eddie said. "You are not following J.J."

"We're not?" Liza asked.

Eddie shook his head. "You are going to follow me," Eddie told them. "And you are going to cheer louder than every kid in Bailey City because I am going to win the contest."

Eddie didn't wait for his friends to agree. Howie, Liza, and Melody hurried after Eddie as he headed straight for the contest.

Kids were already in line when they got there. Each kid in the contest got three tries using a huge mallet to hit a giant target. The kid that hit the hardest would be named the Strongest Kid in Bailey City.

With each hit, the scales clanged. An alarm beeped louder and louder. The crowd cheered and cheered. Everybody yelled. Everyone but Howie. He was too busy spying on J.J. She was standing at the back of the crowd. One hand held her giant umbrella and she used her other hand to cover one ear as the noise grew even louder.

Several kids took their turn, but finally the contest came down to Ben and Eddie.

Eddie glared at Ben. "This will prove once and for all," Eddie told the fourth-grade bully, "that I am the strongest kid in Bailey City."

Ben puffed out his chest. "You're wrong," he said. "I'm the biggest, the meanest, and the strongest. Just wait and see!"

"Eddie! Eddie! EDDIE!" chanted half the crowd.

The rest of the group started yelling, "Ben! Ben! BEN!"

Ben stepped up and grabbed the mallet. He held it high over his head. Then he slammed it into the target. The crowd roared as the bells clanged and the alarm rang out across the carnival park. It was the strongest hit yet.

"Your turn, weakling," Ben said with a laugh. Then he tossed the mallet at Eddie.

Eddie caught the mallet with one hand and stepped toward the target. He glared at Ben. "Get ready to lose," Eddie said to Ben, "because I'm going to hit that target so hard, the alarms will burst your eardrums!"

That's when Howie heard something that sent shivers up his spine. A wicked laugh was coming straight from J.J.

"Oh, no," Howie gasped. He grabbed Melody's and Liza's arms, pulling them away from the cheering crowd so they could hear.

"J.J.'s planning to silence the Strongest Kid contest," he told his two friends.

"But if she silences the contest," Liza said, "that can mean only one thing."

"It means," Melody said, "that Eddie will lose!"

12

Strongest Kid

Eddie lifted the mallet over his head. A huge group of third-graders cheered for Eddie. "Go, Eddie!" they screamed.

"Look at J.J.," Liza said. "She has her fingers in her ears." J.J. held her umbrella in the crook of her arm and had both ears covered.

Howie sighed. "I'm afraid she's going to ruin Eddie's chances. Trolls will do anything to stop noise."

"I guess it's hopeless," Melody said. "We tried to stop J.J., but we failed."

Liza didn't listen. She rushed over to J.J. before her friends could stop her. Liza stared at J.J.'s bright green eyes and windblown hair.

J.J. took her fingers out of her ears and

frowned at Liza. "What do you want?" J.J. squeaked.

Liza gulped. "I just want to tell you that Eddie really likes you."

J.J. shrugged and continued frowning. Liza kept on talking. "If the bell is silenced on the scales, Eddie can't win."

"So?" J.J. grumbled. "Why should I care?"

Liza didn't give up, even though J.J. looked mad enough to bite off a snake's head. "If Eddie loses, it will ruin his entire day."

J.J. didn't look very convinced, so Liza kept on trying. "If Eddie loses, he'll be so unhappy he'll probably cry all day long. Eddie is really LOUD when he cries."

J.J. looked at Liza. Then J.J. looked at the screaming crowd and Eddie. J.J. put her fingers in her ears just as Eddie smashed the mallet into the target.

Bells rang and sirens blasted. The scales dinged and the crowd cheered. "You did it!" Howie said, running up beside Eddie and slapping him on the back.

Eddie pumped his arms up and posed for the crowd. "I'm the strongest kid around," he said with a grin.

Liza turned to thank J.J., but she was too late. J.J. had disappeared without a trace. Liza and Melody rushed over to Eddie to congratulate him.

"I can't believe J.J. let you win," Melody told Eddie.

"J.J. likes you," Liza told Eddie. "She didn't want to ruin your day."

Eddie rolled his eyes. "J.J. didn't have anything to do with it," he said. "I did it all by myself."

Ben came up to Eddie and put his hand on his shoulder. Liza almost fainted. "Don't beat up Eddie," Liza told Ben.

Ben grinned. "Maybe another day. I just wanted to congratulate him. He won fair and square. Right now I'm going to ride the Monster."

"We can't," Eddie said sadly as Ben left. "It's still broken."

Just then a loud roar sounded from nearby and Eddie broke into a big smile. "That's the Monster and it's fixed."

"Of course it is," Howie said. "J.J. did a good deed by letting Eddie win the contest. She earned her belly-button jewel and now she can do all kinds of good deeds, like fixing the roller coaster."

Liza smiled. "Good deeds really make the world a better place."

Eddie shrugged. "I don't know about that, but I do know one thing."

"What?" Liza, Melody, and Howie asked together.

"Roller coasters make the carnival my favorite place in Bailey City!" Eddie yelled as he raced toward the Monster.

About the Authors

Debbie Dadey and Marcia Thornton Jones have fun writing stories together. When they both worked at an elementary school in Lexington, Kentucky, Debbie was the school librarian and Marcia was a teacher. During their lunch break in the school cafeteria, they came up with the idea of the Bailey School Kids.

Debbie and her family live in Fort Collins, Colorado. Marcia and her husband still live in Kentucky.

Don't miss these

The

BAILEY SCHOOL KIDS

Special Editions!